The Wishing Well

Om KIDZ
An imprint of Om Books International

Om KIDZ | Om Books International

Reprinted in 2023

Corporate & Editorial Office
A-12, Sector 64, Noida 201 301
Uttar Pradesh, India
Phone: +91 120 477 4100
Email: editorial@ombooks.com
Website: www.ombooksinternational.com

ISBN: 978-93-52760-36-7

Printed in India

10 9 8 7 6 5 4 3 2

Sales Office
107, Ansari Road, Darya Ganj
New Delhi 110 002, India
Phone: +91 11 4000 9000
Email: sales@ombooks.com
Website: www.ombooks.com

The Wishing Well

Paste your photograph here

My name is

In a faraway **village,** lives a man.
He **works very** hard.

He **walks** around the **village,** selling **vegetables** every day of the **week.**

He carries his **vegetables** in a **wheelbarrow.** Even if the **weather** is bad, he still goes to work.

The **vegetable** seller is **very** poor. His shoes are torn. His feet get cold **when** it is **wet.** He doesn't have a lot of money or food.

One **winter**, the **vegetable** seller **walks** to the **village.**

As he is on his **way**,
he begins to feel **weak.**

He has to cross a **wild** forest
on his **way** to the **village.**
There is a cold **wind.** It is dark.
The man gets lost in the forest.

Suddenly he reaches a **well.**

He **waits** and rests near the **well.**

He drinks the **water** from the **well.**

He sees the **village** in the distance. He sees the houses **with** brightly lit **windows.** The houses look **warm.**

"I am freezing," says the **vegetable** seller. "I **wish** it was not so cold."

Suddenly he hears a **voice** coming from the **well** – "Your **wish will** be granted."

The **vegetable** seller suddenly feels **warm.** He realises that the **well** has granted his **wish.**

The **vegetable** seller **wonders** **what** else he can **wish** for. A **warm** house? A shop?

He can **wish** for
whatever he **wants.**

He **wishes** for food!

For he is **very** hungry.

Suddenly a lot of food appears. There is soup, fruit, bread and cheese. The man **washes** his hands **with** the **well water.** He eats the food till his tummy is full.

The **vegetable** seller is never hungry again. The **wishing well** gives him **whatever** he needs. He becomes rich with a pretty **wife** and a lovely house. He lives happily ever after.

Know your words

Naming words

village
wheelbarrow
wind
voice
winter
well
vegetable
way
water
week
windows
wife

Describing words

wet
wild
warm
weak

Doing words

walks
wishes
wants
waits
wonders

Sight words

very
without
whatever
weather

Circle the words beginning with 'w'.

week
soon
wish
seller
rich
window
cold
walk
well
keep
wear

Spot 5 differences between the given pictures.

Join the dots to show something that carries vegetables. Colour it.